TIGERS IN TERAI

ADVENTURES OF RILEY

BY AMANDA LUMRY
& LAURA HURWITZ

EAGLEMONT
Press

ILLUSTRATED BY
SARAH MCINTYRE

We dedicate this book to the people of Nepal and India, the tigers of the Terai, and to a future in which both can thrive.

All photographs by Amanda Lumry except:
pg. 9 peafowl, pg. 24 sloth bear, and cover inset langur monkey family by Art Wolfe/Art Wolfe, Inc.;
pg. 3 Tiger Tops Airport by Grayce Roessier/Indexstock;
pg. 17 clouded leopard © Tom and Pat Leeson/Imagestate;
pg. 27 Bengal tiger by John Shaw/Bruce Coleman Inc.;
cover inset Bengal tiger by Karen McDonald/Bruce Coleman, Inc.

Illustrations ©2003 by Sarah McIntyre
Editing and Finished Layouts by Michael E. Penman

Digital Imaging by Embassy Graphics, Canada
Printed in China by Midas Printing International Limited

Library of Congress Control Number: 2002115178

ISBN: 0-9662257-7-5

A portion of the proceeds from your purchase of this licensed product supports the stated educational mission of the Smithsonian Institution - "the increase and diffusion of knowledge." The name of the Smithsonian Institution and the sunburst logo are registered trademarks of the Smithsonian Institution and are registered in the U.S. Patent and Trademark Office.
www.si.edu

2% of the proceeds from this book will be donated to the Wildlife Conservation Society.
http://wcs.org

A royalty of approximately 1% of the estimated retail price of this book will be received by World Wildlife Fund (WWF). The Panda Device and WWF are registered trademarks. All rights reserved by World Wildlife Fund, Inc.
www.worldwildlife.org

First edition published 2003
by Eaglemont Press
PMB 741
15600 NE 8th #B-1
Bellevue, WA 98008
(425) 462-6618
info@eaglemontpress.com
www.eaglemontpress.com

A special thank you to all the scientists who collaborated on this project. Your assistance was invaluable.

Dear Riley,

Greetings, Carrot Top! Your Aunt Martha, Cousin Alice and I are so excited you could join us in Nepal. We have some detective work to do!

Like tigers everywhere, the tigers in the Terai region of Nepal and India are endangered. To save the tigers, they require more space to roam. We must find them and study their habits, so we can figure out ways for them to survive.

Be sure to bring a camera and binoculars, since tigers are tricky to spot! I am counting on you and Alice to be my extra sets of eyes, since you know my poor eyesight!

Your favourite scientist,

Uncle Max

1

"Welcome to Kathmandu!" laughed Uncle Max.

"It's so good to see you!" said Riley. "I have never seen mountains taller than the clouds."

"We are in the Himalayas, the highest mountain range in the world. Take in the view, Carrot Top. We have a flight to catch to the lowlands of the Terai."

2

After landing, they were greeted by people selling crafts. A painted wooden tiger caught Riley's eye.

"Riley! Alice!" called Uncle Max from the car. "Time to go! Hey, I'm glad to see you have already spotted a tiger. Keep up the good work!"

Soon their car reached a river.

"Do we get to ride in a boat?" asked Alice.

"Hop in!" said Uncle Max.

"No hopping, Max," said Aunt Martha.
"We don't want to tip over. You never know
where the crocodiles are hiding!"

Uncle Max gave Riley a toothy grin.

Once they reached the other side, they took a Jeep to the lodge.

A young woman named Penny showed them around the jungle camp. "It is a pleasure to have you back, Professor Maxwell. Your knowledge of camera traps and scientific samples can help us locate and study our tigers."

Their rooms were made of woven reeds.

"It sure is hot in here. I am going to open a window," said Aunt Martha.

"So, what are we going to do now?" Riley asked as he and Alice jumped onto the bed.

"We could unpack, or..." Uncle Max said with a twinkle in his eye, "we could ride an elephant."

"Yeah!!" Alice and Riley yelled.

6

At the loading platform, a nervous Riley and Alice carefully climbed onto a very large elephant. They had to hang on tightly because the elephant swayed back and forth as it walked.

"My name is Mohan," said the guide in front, "and this is Kanchi the elephant."

ASIAN ELEPHANT

➤ Two times around an elephant's footprint is equal to its height.

➤ They use their trunks and feet to "hear" sounds through the ground made by other elephants.

➤ Elephants feed for 16 hours a day.

Eric Wikramanayake
Senior Conservation
Scientist
World Wildlife Fund

"What a challenging job this must be!" said Aunt Martha.

"Yes! I have always loved elephants and now I live with one," Mohan said.

"What? You live with an elephant?" gasped Alice. "That's so funny!"

"Well, not really. Trainers must live near the elephants so they can care for them in the middle of the night," explained Mohan.

Suddenly, they heard what sounded like someone yelling for help.

"Oh, no! Someone's in trouble!" cried Riley.

"Don't worry, Riley," said Mohan. "That is just a peafowl calling."

Riley quickly took a picture, while Alice laughed and wrote about Riley's little scare in her journal.

PEAFOWL

➤ Males attract females with their blue bodies and long colorful tail feathers that form a fan.

➤ Males do not help at all with nest building or taking care of the young.

➤ Even though they feed on the ground, they fly up into the trees to sleep.

John Morrison
Senior Conservation Specialist
World Wildlife Fund

Mohan urged Kanchi through the tall reeds.

"Riley, quit bumping into me!" said Alice.

"It's not my fault. Every time the elephant takes a step, I get pushed into you."

"Shhh! I think I see a rhinoceros up ahead," whispered Uncle Max.

"Are you sure it's not a tiger?" joked Riley, remembering his Uncle's bad eyesight.

"Don't give your uncle such a hard time! It is a greater Asian one-horned rhinoceros," said Mohan.

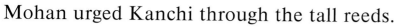

RHINOCEROS

➤ They have poor eyesight (just like Uncle Max!) so they use their sense of smell to get around.

➤ Males mark their territory by peeing in key locations.

➤ They hold the world's record for the single largest poop.

Eric Dinerstein, Chief Scientist, Vice President for Science, World Wildlife Fund

Back at camp they ate dinner and went to their rooms.
"What happened to my suitcase?" exclaimed Uncle Max.
"Nothing seems to be missing except for my sample
containers. We cannot study the tiger population without something
to collect dung and hair samples properly. Now what will I do?!"

11

After breakfast, they met Penny to look for the missing containers and check on the camp's camera traps. Mishra, Mohan's younger brother who helped out at the camp, joined the search.

They stopped in front of a camera trap tied to a tree.

"How does it work?" Riley asked.

"This camera takes pictures by itself whenever an animal walks in front of it. The pictures will show me which tigers, if any, are in this area."

"Why are those big black birds hanging upside down?" Alice asked.

"Actually, those are not birds. They are Indian Flying Foxes," said Uncle Max.

"What, are you crazy? Foxes can't fly!" Riley laughed.

"That's true," said Uncle Max, "but these are not foxes. They are really bats and that is why they are hanging upside down."

INDIAN FLYING FOX

➤ Weighing over 1 pound/0.5kg and with a wingspan of four feet, they are one of the largest bats.

➤ They are good at remembering the location of fruit trees and when the fruit is ripe.

➤ They do not eat the fruit itself, only the juice.

Don E. Wilson
Senior Scientist
Smithsonian
Institution

"Shhh," said Mishra. "Over there are some Chital deer and they get scared easily."

"Mishra, you make a first-rate guide!" whispered Uncle Max.

"Thanks. That is what I want to be when I grow up, but I am afraid of tigers."

"Why?" asked Alice.

"Tigers killed some of the goats my family raises to sell."

"Oh, that's so horrible!" said Alice.

"I am working to solve those kinds of problems," said Uncle Max. "By making more space for tigers to roam, they will stay away from people and increase in number at the same time."

"I am sure this will be good news for the goats!" Aunt Martha grinned.

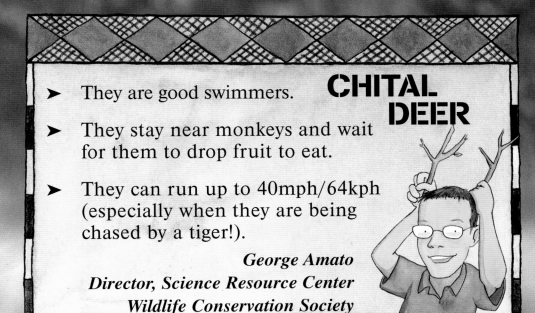

CHITAL DEER

➤ They are good swimmers.

➤ They stay near monkeys and wait for them to drop fruit to eat.

➤ They can run up to 40mph/64kph (especially when they are being chased by a tiger!).

George Amato
Director, Science Resource Center
Wildlife Conservation Society

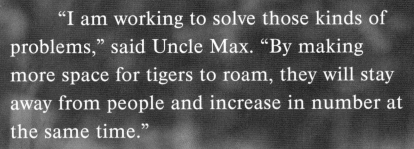

"Hey Dad," called Alice. "That monkey is wearing your underwear!" Uncle Max burst out laughing. "That must be the little rascal who sneaked in and made a mess of my suitcase!"

As the monkey ran off, Riley noticed Uncle Max's sample containers. He climbed up and was just the right size to squeeze through the branches to rescue them. "Riley, you saved the day!" beamed Uncle Max.

HANUMAN LANGUR MONKEY

➤ They enjoy spending time together in large groups.

➤ They can leap 33 feet/10m high and 16 feet/5m across.

➤ They have only one baby at a time.

Dr. Cathi Lehn
Conservation Biologist
Science Resource Center
Wildlife Conservation Society

16

CLOUDED LEOPARD

➤ They are the smallest member of the big cats.

➤ Their name comes from the "cloudy" dark patches on their fur.

➤ They stay in tree branches away from danger (tigers).

Louise Emmons
Research Associate,
Systematic
Biology
Smithsonian
Institution

On their way back to camp, Uncle Max caught a glimpse of a dark shape hidden in a nearby tree. He pulled out his binoculars.

"What is it? A baby tiger?" asked a curious Riley.

"No," whispered Uncle Max. "This is a clouded leopard. It is a very rare sighting, even more unusual than a tiger! Be sure to take a picture and jot it down in your journal."

Clouded leopard 1
Hanuman langur 4711
monkey
Peafowl 1
Chital deer 1111
rhino 1
Asian el.

17

They ate lunch and rushed to the river's edge to watch the trainers give the elephants their daily bath.

What a sight it was!

The elephants helped by using their trunks to rinse themselves off.

"Fascinating!" said Uncle Max as he leaned closer – *maybe too close.* Just then, he was sprayed all over by a baby elephant!

"I guess you will not need a shower today!" giggled Alice.

As Riley waited for everyone to dry off and catch up, he noticed a small pouch under a bush. It was full of coins and he quickly stuck it in his pocket. He could not believe his luck. Now he had money to buy the carved tiger!

Continuing the elephant ride, Uncle Max asked Mohan to stop at a tree with fresh tiger claw scratches. Uncle Max showed them how to pick up the dung and hair the tiger left behind. "The hair helps me learn which tiger it was and whether it was a male or female, while the dung tells me what it ate."

"It sure is stinky!" sniffed Alice.

> Tigers do not live in Africa. One can find them in the hot, tropical forests of southern Asia and the cold, arctic plains of Siberia.

> Tigers are the largest member of the cat family (including lions).

Dr. Anup Joshi
Ecologist
World Wildlife Fund

TIGERS

That night Riley dreamed of tigers.

21

In the morning, they went on another jungle walk with Penny. Riley and Alice found more tiger hair samples for Uncle Max.

"Hey, what is that loud noise?" asked Riley. "This time I *know* it is not a person."

"That's a Great Indian Hornbill," Penny said, "and it is announcing its territory. Or perhaps there is danger nearby."

22

KING COBRA

➤ At 16ft/5m, these are the longest poisonous snakes in the world.

➤ They can kill an elephant with one bite.

➤ They are very good at catching and eating other snakes.

John Behler
Curator of Herpetology
Wildlife Conservation
Society

"Um...is that danger over there?" Alice whispered. A giant snake raised its head off the ground and stared at them.

Uncle Max shouted, "KING COBRA!" He rushed everyone out of the way.

23

Deciding it was safer to drive than walk, they went out in a Jeep to replace the batteries and film in the camera traps. A little way up the road, they crossed paths with a sloth bear. It was almost close enough to touch – *good thing they were in the Jeep!*

➤ They suck insects into their mouths through a space between their teeth. (That's worse than slurping your soup!)

➤ These sounds can be heard from 330ft/100m away.

➤ They have paler fur on their chest in the shape of a "U", "V" or "Y."

Robert S. Hoffmann
Senior Scientist
Smithsonian Institution

SLOTH BEAR

Later they stopped so Uncle Max could
check a camera trap.

"Uncle Max, is that tiger dung?" Riley said,
pointing to a fresh pile.

"Why yes! That's great, Riley!" said Uncle Max.
"I sure hope this film has lots of tiger shots," he
muttered to himself.

25

"Dad!" gulped Alice.

"T-T-Tiger! There's a tiger behind you!"

At the sound of Alice's voice, the big cat looked up at her.

Uncle Max leapt into the front seat...JUST IN TIME!

They held their breath as the tiger slowly crept past the Jeep, then seemed to melt back into the grass.

Whew! Uncle Max cautiously went back and picked up the tiger dung.

"Thanks to all of you," Uncle Max said, "this is the best tiger spotting trip I have had in a long time! We have lots of data, which will help with our research as we work to make a bigger home for tigers. I believe that there is hope for them, but we need to keep working."

TIGERS

➤ Tigers can eat up to 90 pounds/40kg of meat at one time.

➤ They have black stripes to help them blend in when they are in tall grass or dark forests.

Dr. Alan Rabinowitz
Director of Science
and Exploration

Wildlife Conservation
Society

Riley and Alice were still shaking from their close call with the tiger. At camp, they ran to find Mohan and Mishra.

"We saw a tiger!" Riley said. Mishra tried to smile, but he couldn't.

"What's wrong?" asked Alice.

"I lost my money pouch. My parents count on me to help out," said Mishra.

Riley thought for a second then reached into his pocket. "Is this your pouch? I found it by the river."

"Yes! Thank you!" said a happy Mishra. "But wait! Let me repay your kindness." He quickly ran off and returned, handing Riley a painted wooden tiger just like the one at the airstrip and to Alice a carved beaded necklace.

"Wow, this is just what I wanted," Riley said.

"My father makes these and I help him paint them," said Mishra.

"Riley! Alice! Time to go!" called Aunt Martha. They said
goodbye and thanked their new friends.

29

On the plane, they all slept soundly.

Back at home Riley entertained
his family with stories of the tiger, Mishra and
even the monkey that stole Uncle Max's underwear. He
made a home for the carved wooden tiger and then
returned to living the life of a nine-year-old...until his
Mom handed him a new letter from Uncle Max.

Where will Riley go next?

Further Information

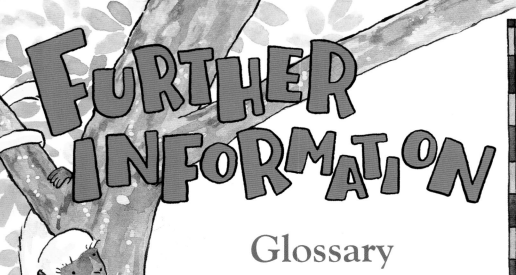

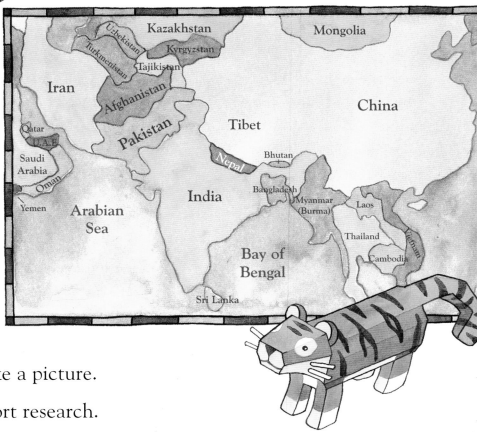

Glossary

camera traps: a camera set up to take pictures without the push of a button - motion in front of the lens makes the camera take a picture.

data: items or things collected to support research.

endangered species: an animal or plant group that is in danger of dying out completely.

research: information about or the process of studying a subject.

sample containers: jars or small tubes used to collect hair, dung or other things that will help scientists find out more about their subjects.

Terai: a region of low-lying land south of the Himalayas in southern Nepal and northern India.

territory: the area that an animal considers its home.

Find the two hidden compass bugs in the story and continue the adventures on-line at www.adventuresofriley.com

The designs on the fact boxes were inspired by the paintings from the Janakpur Women's Development Center in Nepal.

Register your passport at: www.adventuresofriley.com
and explore the planet with Riley!

Come and see what is happening at Riley's World!

Become an Official Member of Riley's World and receive a gold membership sticker for your passport!

Membership is EASY and FREE!

Just go to:

www.adventuresofriley.com

to sign up for loads of fun and educational games, further adventures, and great savings!

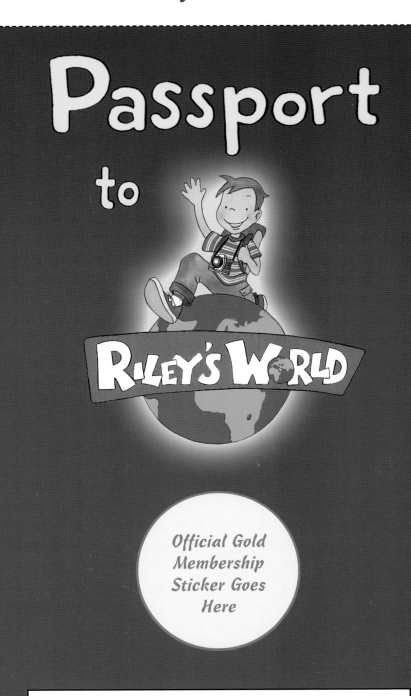

Passport
to

RILEY'S WORLD

Official Gold Membership Sticker Goes Here

Name	Birthday	Date

GET YOUR PASSPORT STAMPED AS YOU TRAVEL THE WORLD WITH RILEY!

Each book contains a unique adventure sticker showing where you visited.

To learn more about Riley and his world join his club at:

www.adventuresofriley.com

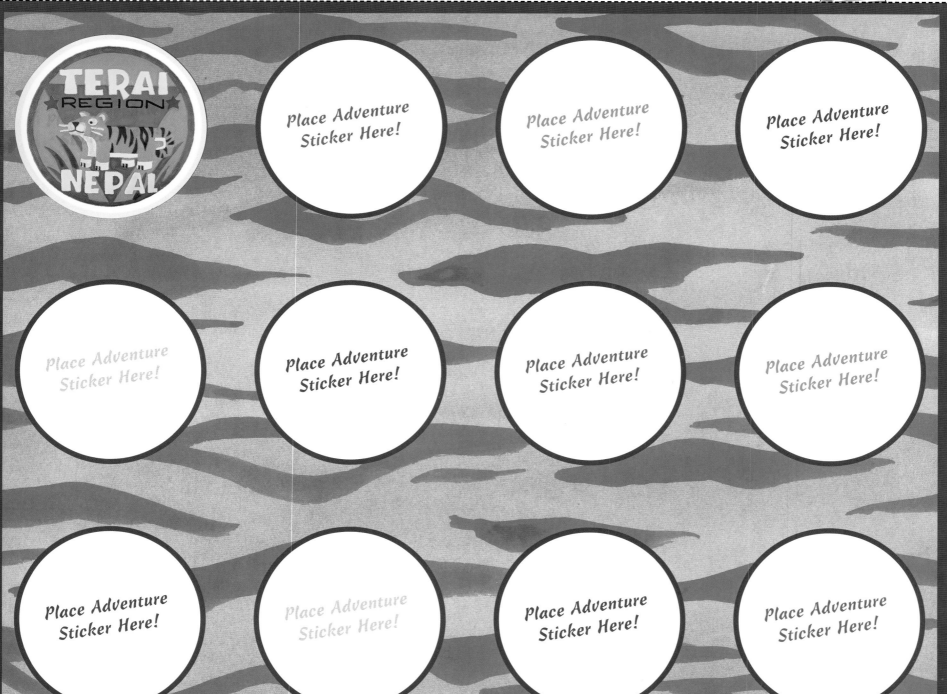

TERAI REGION NEPAL

Place Adventure Sticker Here!

Place Adventure Sticker Here!

Place Adventure Sticker Here!

Place Adventure Sticker Here!

Place Adventure Sticker Here!

Place Adventure Sticker Here!

Place Adventure Sticker Here!

Place Adventure Sticker Here!

Place Adventure Sticker Here!

Place Adventure Sticker Here!

Place Adventure Sticker Here!